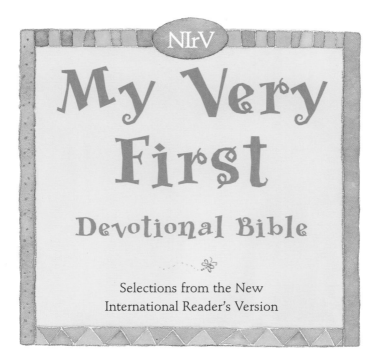

NIrV

My Very First

Devotional Bible

Selections from the New
International Reader's Version

Zonderkidz
The Children's Group of ZondervanPublishingHouse

To Bryce with love from Mom
C. D. V.

With love and gratitude to my husband, Kelly
and my parents, Lora and Winston
L. M. L.

My Very First Devotional Bible
Text copyright © 1999 by Catherine DeVries
Illustrations copyright © 1999 by Leanne Mebust Luetkemeyer

Requests for information should be addressed to:

Zonder**kidz**
The Children's Group of ZondervanPublishingHouse
Grand Rapids, Michigan 49530
www.Zonderkidz.com

Zonderkidz is a trademark of the Zondervan Corporation

Library of Congress Cataloging–in–Publication Data
DeVries, Catherine
My Very First Devotional Bible / by Catherine DeVries; illustrated by Leanne Mebust Luetkemeyer
     p. cm.
     ISBN 0-310-93251-3

99-075813
CIP

This edition printed on acid-free paper and meets the American National Standards Institute Z39.48 standard.

Printed in China

05 06 / ❖ HK/ 10 9 8 7 6 5

To: _____

From: _____

My Very First Devotional Bible

Table of Contents

God Made the World

There once was a boy who loved to go to his grandma's house. And one of the things they liked doing together was making finger paintings. They would paint pictures of people, animals, flowers, and many other things. After their pictures were dry, they would tape them to Grandma's refrigerator for everyone to see.

In the beginning, God created the heavens and the earth.

Genesis 1:1

Read All About It:
Genesis 1:1–31

7

At the very beginning of time, God decided to make something. First God made the sun, moon, and stars. Then he made dry ground, plants, and trees. Then he made all the animals—big, floppy-eared elephants, small, scurrying ants, tall giraffes, and tiny

8

kittens. Finally, God made two people—a man named Adam and a woman named Eve. It took God 1 2 3 4 5 6 days to make the world and everything in it.

How wonderful it is to live in such a beautiful world! God's creation is here for all of us to see!

Idea

Name two or three things God made
when he created the world.

Verse to Remember

"In the beginning,
God created the heavens
and the earth."

Genesis 1:1

I Shouldn't Hide the Truth

There once was a boy who played ball in the house, even though his mom had told him not to. One day his ball bounced into a lamp and—*crash!* The lamp broke.

The woman . . . took some of the fruit and ate it. She also gave some to her husband. And he ate it. They hid from the LORD. The LORD God said to Adam, "You ate the fruit of the tree that I commanded you about." So the LORD God drove the man out of the Garden of Eden.

Genesis 3:6, 8, 17, 23

Read All About It:
Genesis 3:1–24

He tried to hide what he had done. But soon his mom found out the truth. She punished her little boy for disobeying and for breaking the lamp. But then she wiped his tears and told him that she still loved him . . . even though he had done a bad thing.

In this Bible story, Adam and Eve did not listen to God. He had told them not to eat the fruit from one special tree. But they ate it anyway—*crunch!*

Adam and Eve hid from God because they were afraid. But God already knew the truth. God punished Adam and Eve for disobeying and for eating from the tree. But he still loved them . . . even though they had done a bad thing.

Prayer

Dear God,

I'm sorry I don't always listen
Or do the things I should.
Please help me to follow
you better,
And help me to do
what is good.

Amen.

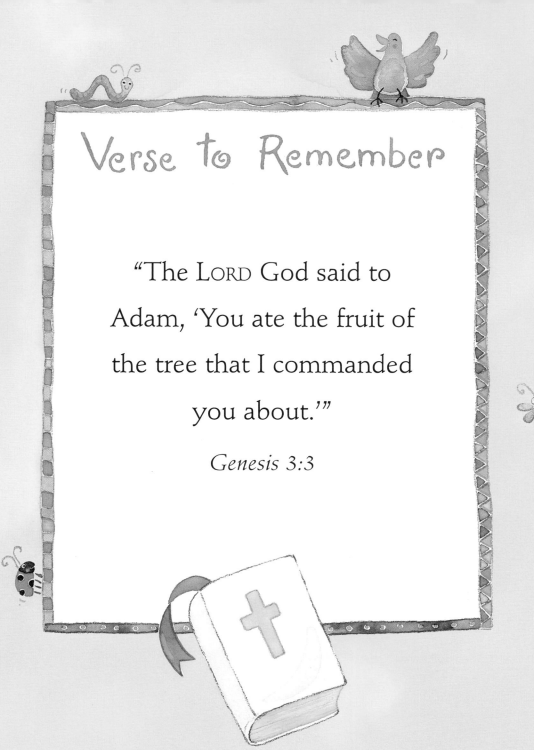

Verse to Remember

"The LORD God said to Adam, 'You ate the fruit of the tree that I commanded you about.'"

Genesis 3:3

Noah Had a Zoo!

Have you ever been to the zoo? What animal do you like to watch the most? The monkeys—*Oo, oo, oo*—how they love to chase each other and play! The elephants walk r-e-a-l-l-y slow, swaying their trunks back and forth. And the lions open their mouths and yawn—what big teeth they have! In the zoo, we see many animals all in one place.

Noah did everything the LORD commanded him to do. He and his [family] entered the ark . . . to escape the waters of the flood. So did pairs of birds and pairs of all of the creatures that move along the ground. Rain fell on the earth for 40 days and 40 nights.

Genesis 7:5, 7–8

Read All About It:
Genesis 6:9—8:12

19

This Bible story reminds us of the zoo. God told Noah to bring two of every kind of animal onto the ark. Can you imagine how loud the animals were, making all their different animal sounds all day long? Imagine roosters crowing, cows mooing, cats purring, dogs barking, bears growling, crickets chirping and frogs croaking . . . all at the same time!

Noah and his family took care of the
animals inside the ark until they could
safely go outside again.

God loved Noah, his family, and all the
animals very much.

Song

Tune: "Old Mac Donald"

Good man Noah had an ark, E-I-E-I-O
And on that ark there were two _____ (cows, cats, dogs, bears, frogs)
With a _____, _____ here (moo, meow, ruff, grrr, ribbet)
And a _____, _____ there (moo, meow, ruff, grrr, ribbet)
Here a _____, there a _____, (moo, meow, ruff, grrr, ribbet)
Everywhere a _____, _____, (moo, meow, ruff, grrr, ribbet)
Good man Noah had an ark, E-I-E-I-O.

Verse to Remember

"Noah did everything
the LORD commanded
him to do."

Genesis 7:5

The Very First Rainbow

Look at this picture of a rainbow. See all the bright colors? There are bands of red and orange and yellow and green. And blue and purple too! Have you ever seen a rainbow peek through the clouds after a rainstorm?

Rainbows are *soooo* big and *soooo* pretty. They start in one place and arch way over to another place. Don't you wish you could touch one?

[God said to Noah,] I have put my rainbow in the clouds. It will be the sign of the covenant between me and the earth. Sometimes when I bring clouds over the earth, a rainbow will appear in them. Then I will remember my covenant between me and you and every kind of living thing.

Genesis 9:13–15

Read All About It: Genesis 9:8–15

Did you know that the Bible tells us the story of the very first rainbow? God put a rainbow in the sky as a sign to Noah. God promised he would never again send a flood of water that would cover the whole world.

When you see a rainbow, you can remember the promise God made to Noah long ago.

Idea

Pretend that you are a rainbow. Sit
down and put your hands and feet
on the floor. Now arch your back!

Verse to Remember

"'I have put my rainbow
in the clouds.'"

Genesis 9:13

A Beautiful Robe

A boy's grandma wanted to make something very special for him. She wanted it to remind him of how much she loved him. She decided to knit him a sweater. When she gave the sweater to her grandson, she said, "Imagine that this warm sweater is me giving you a hug every time you wear it." The boy loved the sweater. It was his favorite thing to wear.

Israel loved Joseph more than any of his other sons. Joseph had been born to him when he was old. Israel made him a beautiful robe.

Genesis 37:3

Read All About It: Genesis 37:1–11

Do you have a favorite sweater, or jacket, or shirt that you like to wear? We know from this Bible verse that Joseph had a favorite article of clothing to wear. It was his robe. Joseph loved his robe because his father made it just for him. Whenever he wore the robe, he could imagine that it was his father giving him a hug. What colors do you see in Joseph's beautiful robe?

Idea

Put on your bathrobe or coat and pretend you are Joseph. Describe all of the different colors in your beautiful "robe."

Verse to Remember

"Israel made him a
beautiful robe."

Genesis 37:3

I Forgive You

How do you feel when your friends or family members are mean to you? Kind of sad, right? Sometimes people wait a long time before they say they're sorry. In fact, they might not *ever* say they're sorry. Still, you need to forgive people who hurt you. That takes a lot of love!

Joseph said to his brothers . . . "I am your brother Joseph. I'm the one you sold into Egypt. But don't be upset. God sent me . . . here to save your lives."

Genesis 45:4–5, 7

Forgive, just as the Lord forgave you.

Colossians 3:13

Read All About It: Genesis 37:19–28, 45:1–7

In this Bible story, Joseph's brothers were very mean to him. Remember what they did? They sold him as a slave. But God helped Joseph. Joseph became a very famous and powerful man in the country of Egypt. He lived in the palace with the pharaoh (the pharaoh was the king).

When the people in the land had no food, Joseph's brothers traveled to Egypt and asked for his help. Joseph could have been mean to his brothers after what they did to him. But Joseph gave them the food they needed. And he decided to forgive his brothers. That took a lot of love!

Idea

The next time someone is mean to you, remember Joseph's story. And remember to be kind to your friends and family members too!

Verse to Remember

"Forgive, just as the Lord
forgave you."

Colossians 3:13

I Can Float!

When it's time to go swimming, you usually wear "floaties" or a life preserver, right? These things help you keep your head above the water. It's fun to float on your back. Oops, someone just splashed you! Sometimes you sit on top of an inner tube or a rubber raft. You float this way and that way, drifting wherever the water takes you.

[Moses' mother] got a basket that was made out of the stems of tall grass. She coated it with tar. Then she placed the child in it. She put the basket in the tall grass that grew along the bank of the Nile River. Pharaoh's daughter . . . saw the basket in the tall grass. He became her son.

Exodus 2:3, 5, 10

Read All About It:
Exodus 2:1–10

43

In this Bible story, baby Moses needed to be kept away from wicked Pharaoh. Moses' mother helped him get away safely. She set him in a basket on a river. Baby Moses floated this way and that way, drifting wherever the water took him. Moses' sister, Miriam, watched from the river's edge.

A princess saw the basket as it floated
by. When she looked inside and saw baby
Moses, she decided he should live in the
royal palace with her. And, as his mother
had hoped, God watched over Moses and
kept him safe.

Song

(Traditional)

He's got the whole world in his hands. (4 times)

He's got the little bitty baby in his hands, (3 times)

  he's got the whole world in his hands.

He's got you and me sister in his hands, (3 times)

  he's got the whole world in his hands.

He's got you and me brother in his hands, (3 times)

  he's got the whole world in his hands.

Verse to Remember

"She put the basket in the
tall grass that grew along
the bank of the Nile River."

Exodus 2:3

Campfires and Burning Bushes

Have you ever sat beside a campfire? The logs on the fire crackle and pop. To keep the fire going, you need to keep adding logs to it. The flames from the fire flicker. But watch out! It's really hot!

It's fun to sit around the fire and think about God—maybe even sing songs to him.

The angel of the LORD appeared to him from inside a burning bush. Moses saw that the bush was on fire. But it didn't burn up. The LORD said, "I have seen my people suffer in Egypt. So now, go. I am sending you to Pharaoh. I want you to bring the Israelites out of Egypt."

Exodus 3:2, 7, 10

Read All About It:
Exodus 3:1–21

In this Bible story, Moses watched a fire too. It was a burning bush. It must have crackled and popped as the flames burned the wood. But you know what? The bush never burned up.

As Moses watched the burning bush, another amazing thing happened. Moses heard a voice. It was God! God talked to Moses from out of the burning bush. He told Moses to help God's people, the Israelites, get away from a place called Egypt. Moses thought about what God had said; then he went to Egypt to help the Israelites.

Idea

Ask your mom or dad (or another adult) to light a candle for you. As you watch the candle flame, think about how Moses felt when God talked to him out of the fire.

Verse to Remember

"The angel of the LORD appeared to him from inside a burning bush. Moses saw that the bush was on fire. But it didn't burn up."

Exodus 3:2

Walking Through the Sea

When we go to the zoo, we see fish and other water animals in big tanks called "aquariums." We watch the fish swish their tails back and forth as they swim. We see crabs scurry along the bottom. We feel like we are swimming because of the water all around us. But we don't even get wet—how fun!

Then Moses reached his hand out over the Red Sea. All that night the LORD pushed the sea back with a strong east wind. He turned the sea into dry land. The people of Israel went through the sea on dry ground. There was a wall of water on their right side and on their left.

Exodus 13:21–22

Read All About It:
Exodus 13:18—14:31

As Moses led the Israelites away from Egypt, wicked Pharaoh chased them. The people stood on the edge of the Red Sea. What were the Israelites going to do?

God helped Moses and the Israelites that day. God split the huge sea into two parts—almost like two big aquariums. As the people walked through, they may have seen fish swishing their tails as they swam. They may have seen crabs scurrying along the bottom. Moses and the Israelites must have felt like they were swimming, but they never even got wet. God helped them get away from wicked Pharaoh. Hurray!

Poem

Pharaoh's army was coming with swords and bows!
Where would the people of Israel go?
As they stood with their feet at the edge of the sea,
They cried out to Moses, "How can this be?"
God helped his people. With a wave of his hand,
The people of Israel walked through on dry land.

Verse to Remember

"The people of Israel went through the sea on dry ground. There was a wall of water on their right side and on their left."

Exodus 13:22

I'm Hungry!

"I'm hungry!" Have you ever said that? Yes, we all have! When you are hungry, your tummy needs food. It might even make rumble grumble noises that mean, "Feed me!" Thank goodness you never have to wait too long before you get something to eat. And you usually have a choice of what you'd like to eat. Peanut butter and jelly sandwiches, apples, pizza, ice cream—what's your favorite thing to eat?

[The people of Israel said to Moses and Aaron,] "You have brought us out into this desert. You must want this entire community to die of hunger." Then the LORD spoke to Moses. He said, "I will rain down bread from heaven for you." The people of Israel called the bread manna.

Exodus 16:3–4, 31

Read All About It:
Exodus 16:1–31

Well, God's people in this Bible story were feeling very hungry. They were on a trip, and they didn't know how long they would be away. Their tummies were making rumble grumble noises that meant, "Feed me!" So they said to God, "We're hungry!" God sent food called "manna" that fell down from the sky like snowflakes. Manna tasted like bread sweetened with honey.

Even in the desert, God took care of his people and fed them every single day. Praise God for food!

Idea

Pretend that you are picking up manna. Break some bread into small pieces. Then sprinkle the pieces on the table. Get a paper bag and pick up all the pieces of bread. Now eat them as part of your lunch.

Verse to Remember

"'I will rain down bread
from heaven for you.'"

Exodus 16:4

I Need to Follow the Rules

Wipe your feet. Don't run in the house. Brush your teeth.

Rules, rules, rules! Sometimes you get kind of tired of them, don't you? But rules are there for a reason. What would happen if you didn't ever wipe your feet? What could get broken if you ran through the house? And what do you think would happen if you never brushed your teeth? Rules help you live the way you should.

Love the Lord your God with all your heart and with all your soul [and] with all your mind. Love your neighbor as you love yourself.

Matthew 22:37–39

Read All About It:
Exodus 20:1–17

God has rules in the Bible too. They are called the Ten Commandments. These rules help us to know how God wants us to live. But do you know what is the most important rule of all? To love God with all of your heart, soul, and mind. The next most important rule is to love others as much as you love yourself. That takes a lot of love, doesn't it?

Song

This is my commandment that you love one another

That your joy may be full (repeat first 2 lines)

That your joy may be full (2 times)

This is my commandment that you love one another

That your joy may be full.

Cheye McRary, Howard McRary, 1978.
Sonlife Music (CCLI 084023)

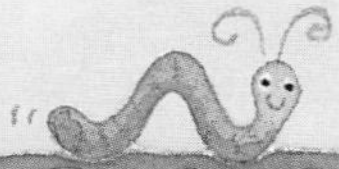

Verse to Remember

"Love the Lord your God
with all your heart and with
all your soul [and] with
all your mind."

Matthew 22:37

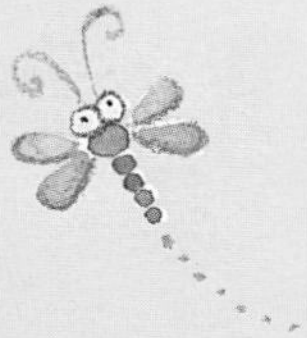

Who Is the Real God?

When we play with puppets, we put our hands inside of them and move our fingers. Then the puppets move. They look like they are alive and talking. But we know that puppets can't talk and that they aren't alive. They only help us play and pretend.

In this Bible story, the people asked Aaron to make them something that they could worship. They believed in other gods besides the one true God.

The people . . . gathered around Aaron. They said to him, "Make us a god that will lead us." Aaron . . . took what they gave him and made it into a metal statue of a god. It looked like a calf. Then the people said, "Israel, here is your god."

Exodus 32:1, 3, 4

Read All About It:
Exodus 32:1–8

Remember those puppets we just talked about? Well, believing in other gods is like believing that those puppets are really alive! But a good man named Moses told the people that they were wrong. He told them that our God is the one and only God. He is the only one we should worship.

Idea

Put a puppet on your hand. Move your fingers and pretend that it's talking. Now take your hand out of the puppet. What happens? Can the puppet still talk? Can it move?

Verse to Remember

"Aaron . . . took what they gave him and made it into a metal statue of a god. It looked like a calf."

Exodus 32:3

All Fall Down

When you build big towers with your blocks, it's fun to knock them down. You pretend you are building a big city. Higher and higher it goes until—*swoosh!*—down the blocks fall with one sweep of your hand.

In this Bible story God helped a man named Joshua knock down the walls of a real city. And Joshua didn't even have to touch them! He listened to what God told him and his army to do.

The LORD spoke to Joshua. He said, "I have handed Jericho over to you. March around the city once. In fact, do it for six days. On the seventh day, march around the city seven times. Have the priests blow the trumpets as you march. [Then] have all the men give a loud shout. The wall of the city will fall down."

Joshua 6:2–5

Read All About It:
Joshua 6:1–20

They walked around the city once a day for six days. As they walked, they blew their trumpets. On the seventh day, they walked around the city seven times. Then God told them to blow their trumpets and make a loud *SHOUT!* As soon as they did, the walls came tumbling down. God is powerful!

Idea

Build up a big tower with your blocks. Now pretend that you are Joshua and his men. Shout and then and knock the blocks down!

Verse to Remember

"The LORD spoke to Joshua.

He said, 'I have handed

Jericho over to you . . .

The wall of the city will

fall down.'"

Joshua 6:2, 5

Strong Samson

Have you ever gone to a barber shop or a salon to get your hair cut? You sit in a big chair that can spin around and go up and down. In the mirror on the wall, you watch the person cut your hair with scissors. *Snip snip* here, *snip snip* there.

When the snipping stops, you see all of your cut hair on the floor in a big pile. How long do you think your hair would get if you never had it cut?

The angel of the LORD . . . said, "You will become pregnant. You will have a son. He must not cut his hair. He will be set apart to God from the day he is born. He will begin to save Israel from the power of the Philistines." Later, the woman had a baby boy. She named him Samson.

Judges 13:3, 5, 24

Read All About It: Judges 13:1–25

This Bible story is about Samson. He never had his hair cut until he was a grown-up. This set Samson apart as being dedicated to God. Can you imagine how long Samson's hair was by the time he grew up?

As long as Samson didn't cut his hair, God made him super strong. With God's help, Samson helped to save the Israelites from the wicked Philistines.

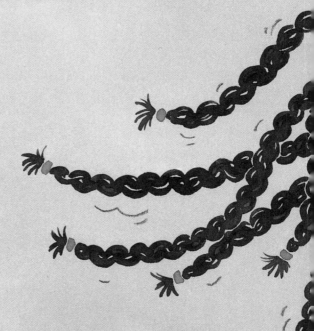

Poem

Samson had hair that was so very long!
As long as he grew it, God made him strong.
When Samson came 'round, the Philistines ran—
They knew God had blessed this mighty man!

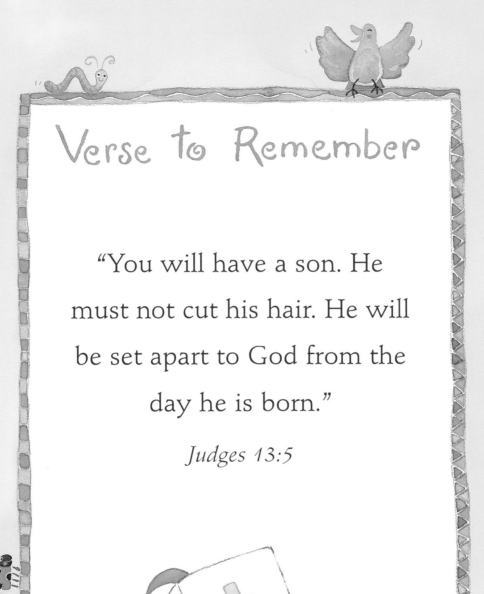

Verse to Remember

"You will have a son. He must not cut his hair. He will be set apart to God from the day he is born."

Judges 13:5

I Have a Job to Do

What job do you want to have when you grow up? Do you want to be a firefighter, or a teacher, or how about an artist? It's fun to think of all of the different kinds of jobs you could have when you grow up.

But guess what? You have a job to do right now! Your job is to love God. Then God wants you to show your love for others by being nice to them, by obeying your parents, and by sharing with your friends. Those things are all part of your job.

Eli realized that the LORD was calling the boy. So Eli told Samuel, "If someone calls out to you again, say, 'Speak, LORD. I'm listening.'" The LORD came and . . . called out, just as he had done the other times. Then Samuel replied, "Speak. I'm listening."

1 Samuel 3:8–10

Read All About It:
1 Samuel 3:1–10

91

In this Bible story, God talked to a boy named Samuel. God had a job for Samuel to do. Samuel listened, and worked as God's prophet for the rest of his life.

See? You don't have to be grown up before you can start working for God. When you do good things for other people, you are doing what God wants you to do.

Idea

Think of one nice thing you can do today for
your mom or dad, for your brother or sister,
or for a friend. Now, go do it!

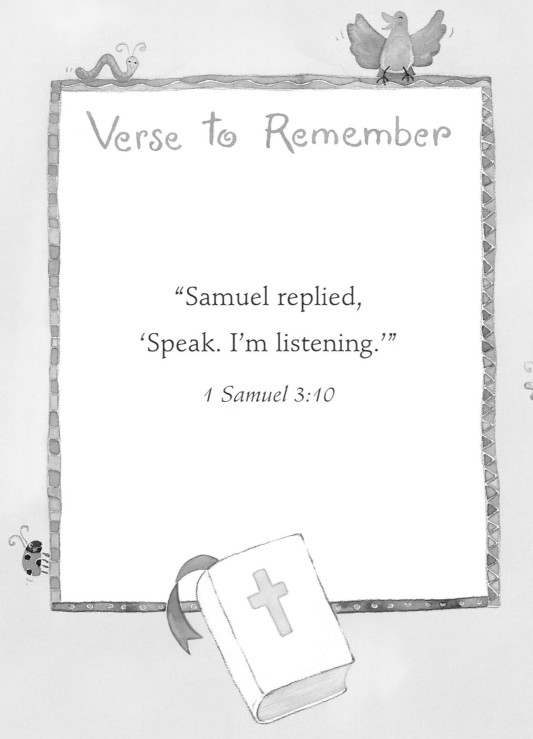

Verse to Remember

"Samuel replied,
'Speak. I'm listening.'"

1 Samuel 3:10

God Can Help Me

Do you ever feel like some things are just too hard to do? How about sitting still during church? That's really hard! Or what about trying to be *shhhh*, quiet when someone else is sleeping? You'd probably rather run around and laugh and giggle and talk talk talk!

Being quiet just isn't much fun. But . . . sometimes you have to do things, even when they are hard to do.

David said to Goliath, "You are coming to fight against me with a sword, a spear and a javelin. But I'm coming against you in the name of the LORD who rules over all . . . This very day the LORD will hand you over to me."

1 Samuel 17:45–46, 49

Read All About It:
1 Samuel 17:1–58

This Bible story is about a boy named David. He needed to do something that was really hard. He had to fight a giant who stood about as high as your bedroom ceiling. Wow, that is really tall!

Was David scared? No! David trusted in God. He didn't let the big giant make him feel afraid. He knew that God would help him. And God did. God helped David knock down the giant with a stone. David won!

Prayer

Dear God,

Please help me remember
That you're always there.
Help me to know
That you'll always care.

When I have to do
Things I think are hard,
Help me to keep
trying—
Keep me going, Lord.

Amen.

Verse to Remember

"I'm coming against you in the name of the LORD who rules over all."

1 Samuel 17:45

Giving Thanks

Long ago, pilgrims sailed across the sea in boats because they wanted to move to America. With the help of the Native Americans, the pilgrims learned how to grow corn, survive snowy winters, protect themselves from wild animals—and much, much more. They were very thankful to God for helping them and giving them everything they needed! They were so thankful that they decided to set aside a whole day just to thank God for his goodness to them.

LORD, you are great and powerful. Everything in heaven and on earth belongs to you. You are honored as the One who rules over all. Our God, we give you thanks. We praise your glorious name.

1 Chronicles 29:11, 13

We still celebrate this day every year. Do you know what it is? Thanksgiving!

Thanksgiving is a wonderful day to spend time with our families around a big dinner.

But the most important thing about Thanksgiving is *giving thanks.* We need to thank God for all the ways he helps us and gives us everything we need. Just as the pilgrims did long ago, we set this day aside so we can thank God for his goodness to us.

Idea

Draw a picture of three things
you are thankful for.

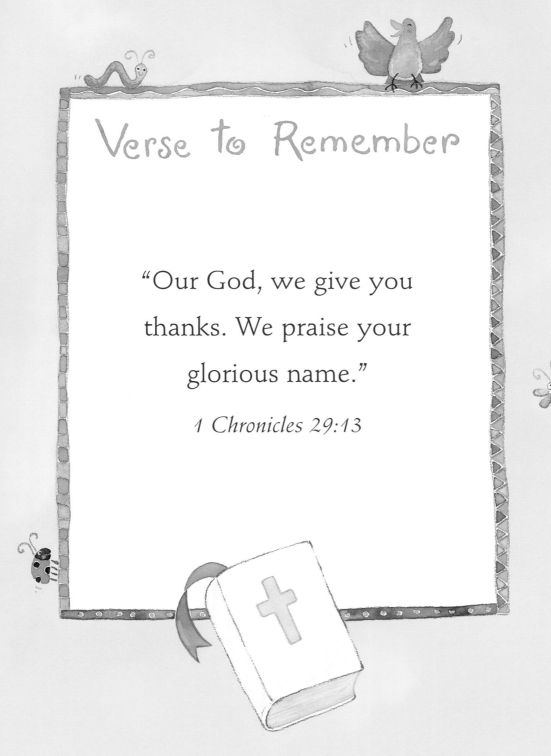

Verse to Remember

"Our God, we give you thanks. We praise your glorious name."

1 Chronicles 29:13

I Want to Sing!

Do you like to sing? What is your favorite song? When are some times that you like to sing?

Well, let's see. You probably sing "Happy Birthday" on someone's birthday. You sing in church. You sing in school. You can even sing in the bathtub, or when you're riding in the car. When you think about it, you can sing just about anywhere!

You have made sure that children and infants praise you.
Psalm 8:2

Sing with joy to the LORD. Sing a new song to him. Play with skill, and shout with joy.
Psalm 33:1, 3

Clap your hands, all you nations. Shout to God with cries of joy. How wonderful is the LORD Most High! He is the great King over the whole earth.
Psalm 47:1–2

Do you know that God loves it when you sing to him? He says so in the Bible. You can praise God and sing to him anytime, anywhere. It's a special way of showing God how happy you are for all the things he has done for you.

110

Song

(Traditional)

If you're happy and you know it, clap your hands. (3 times)

And I'm so happy, so very happy, I have the love of Jesus
in my heart. (repeat)

If you're happy and you know it, stomp your feet. (3 times)

And I'm so happy, so very happy, I have the love of
Jesus in my heart. (repeat)

If you're happy and you know it shout "Amen!"
(3 times)

And I'm so happy, so very happy, I
have the love of Jesus in my
heart. (repeat)

Verse to Remember

"Sing with joy to the LORD."

Psalm 33:1

114

I Love God's World

When it's time for the sun to go down for the day, God puts beautiful colors in the sky. We see yellow, orange, red, pink, purple, and more. After the sun sets and we're tucked in our beds, the moon comes out and shines its light in the night. Sometimes it looks like just a little fingernail, and other times like a round, silver coin. The stars keep the moon company. They twinkle in the nighttime sky. And sometimes they hide behind the clouds.

The heavens tell about the glory of God. The skies show that his hands created them. Day after day they speak about it. Night after night they make it known. But they don't speak or use words.

Psalm 19:1–3

Read All About It:
Psalm 19:1–14

115

116

God made everything in the earth and in the sky. Words can't even describe how wonderful God is. But when we look around and see the wonderful things he has made—like sunsets and silvery, moon-lit nights—we start to understand.

Prayer

God, I thank you for the moon
I thank you for the stars
I thank you the sun and sky
And for this world of yours.

Amen.

Verse to Remember

"The heavens tell about
the glory of God."

Psalm 19:1

Walking With Your Family

Pretend you are going on a walk with your family on a bright, sunny day. You walk to a place with lots of green grass. *Ahh,* how feathery the grass feels—it's as soft as your bed! You roll over onto your tummy and listen to the sounds. What's that bubbling noise? It's a stream!

The LORD is my shepherd. He gives me everything I need. He lets me lie down in fields of green grass. He leads me beside quiet waters. He gives me new strength. He guides me in the right paths for the honor of his name.

Psalm 23:1–3

Read All About It:
Psalm 23:1–6

121

The hours go by as your family enjoys
this peaceful place. Soon the sun is setting.
Your dad turns on a flashlight. You all hold
hands as you find your way back home.

In this passage from the Bible, God
wants us to think of a beautiful place like
this. He wants us to know that he gives us
whatever we need. He lets us lie down in

green fields and walk beside quiet waters.
God is with us wherever we go, whatever
we do. Even when it gets dark outside, we
don't have to be afraid because God is
there with us—always.

Song

(Traditional)

The Lord is my shepherd,
I'll walk with him always.
He leads by still waters,
I'll walk with him always.
Always, always
I'll walk with him
always.
Always, always
I'll walk with him
always.

Verse to Remember

"The LORD is my shepherd.
He gives me everything
I need."

Psalm 23:1

The Lord Is My Lighthouse

Have you ever seen a lighthouse before? Do you know why people build lighthouses that stand on the edge of the water? Well, lighthouses help people who are in boats way out on the water. These people see the light from the lighthouse. They steer their boats toward it so they can get back to land. Without lighthouses, people could get lost because they wouldn't know where to go.

The LORD gives me light and saves me. Why should I fear anyone? The LORD is my place of safety. Why should I be afraid?

Psalm 27:1

God acts like a lighthouse for us. No, he doesn't stand at the edge of the water and flash a light for us to see. But he does watch out for us from heaven. If we ask God for help, he will show us how to live.

How does he show us the way? Through his Word, the Bible. The Bible tells us many things that help us to live as Christians. Without God's help, we wouldn't know how he wants us to live.

Idea

Think about your room at bed time. It's dark, and it's hard to see your closet door or your toys. Then imagine that your mom or dad turns on the hallway light. Now is it easier to see around your room?

Verse to Remember

"The LORD gives me light and saves me. Why should I fear anyone?"

Psalm 27:1

The Farm

Farms are busy places! The cows moo in the morning as they wait for the farmer to milk them. The animals live in a big red barn. Next to the barn is a pasture and a big cornfield. The cows eat the green grass in the pasture. As the days pass, the corn in the field grows up from the ground. Before long, the corn is ready to eat. Do you like to eat corn on the cob? *Munch munch munch!*

You make grass grow for the cattle and plants for people to take care of. That's how they get food from the earth.

Psalm 104:14

Read All About It: Psalm 104:1–31

Corn is just one of many yummy things that grow from the ground. What are some others? Just think of all the food we see at the grocery store or pick from the garden— like peas and carrots, potatoes and tomatoes.

God makes food grow from the ground for animals and people to eat. God wants us to take good care of the animals and the earth. They are all part of his creation.

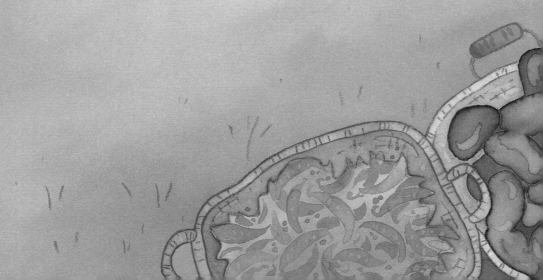

Fresh Vegetables

Prayer

God is great and God is good,
Let us thank him for our food.
By his hand we all are fed,
Let us thank him for our bread.

Amen.

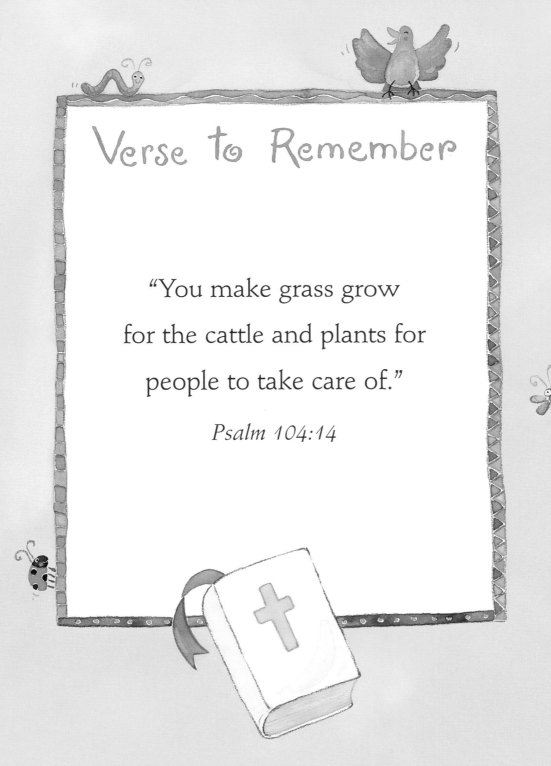

Verse to Remember

"You make grass grow
for the cattle and plants for
people to take care of."

Psalm 104:14

At the Beach

Have you ever been to the beach? The sand feels warm, and it tickles your toes! It's fun to chase the waves. At first the water feels *brrr* so cold, but pretty soon you're splashing and swimming and having so much fun! Then—*ahhhhh*—you lay down on your beach towel. You feel the sun warm you up again, from your toes to your nose—such a nice, sleepy feeling!

LORD, you have made so many things! How wise you were when you made all of them! The earth is full of your creatures. Look at the ocean, so big and wide! It is filled with living things, from the largest to the smallest. May the LORD be happy with what he has made.

Psalm 104:24–25, 31

God made the beautiful beach. He made everything from the sand to the sea gulls. No matter how hard we try, people can't make birds or sand or water. Only God can make these things.

We see how great God is when we see what he makes. The beach is just one small part of God's creation.

We can thank God for all the different parts of nature—like puffy white clouds, red-and-black lady-bugs, trees that stretch way up high, soft little rabbits, and yellow dandelions.

Idea

Look out the window. Do you see
something in nature that you would
like to thank God for today?

Verse to Remember

"May the LORD be happy
with what he has made."

Psalm 104:31

Read the Bible

When your family goes for a ride in the car at night, how does the driver see the road? That's right—with the car's headlights. Without those lights, a driver wouldn't be able to see where he or she was going. Can you imagine trying to stay on the road at night without the lights on? I don't think anyone could do it!

Your word is like a lamp that shows me the way. It is like a light that guides me.

Psalm 119:105

The Bible is kind of like the headlights on a car. When we don't know or can't see what we need to do, we can read the Bible. Just as headlights show us where the road is in the dark, the Bible will show us where God wants us to go and what he wants us to do.

Can you imagine trying to know what God wants us to do without reading the Bible? I don't think anyone could do it!

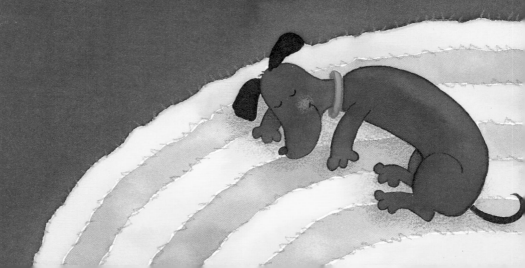

Idea

Cover your eyes with your hands and try
to walk in a straight line for five steps. Turn
around and walk back five steps to where
you began. Now uncover your eyes. Are
you at the same place you
started? Why not?

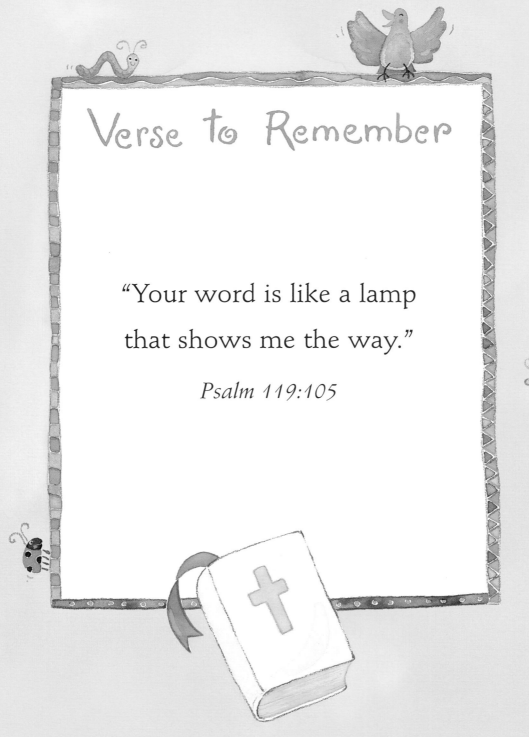

Verse to Remember

"Your word is like a lamp
that shows me the way."

Psalm 119:105

I'm a Present

Do you remember your last birthday? Your family sang "Happy Birthday to you." Then it was time to blow out the candles on your birthday cake and eat a piece. *Mmm . . .* yum. So sweet—what a treat! And do you remember what came next? Yes! Opening all of your birthday presents. Birthdays are so much fun!

Children are a gift from the LORD. They are a reward from him. Children who are born to people when they are young are like arrows in the hands of a soldier. Blessed are those who have many children.

Psalm 127:3–5

But what do you do when it is someone else's birthday? Sometimes it is hard to know what present to give when it's your mom or dad's birthday. They are happy when you draw pictures for them with crayons. And they like it when you give them a great big hug.

But do you know what? You've already given your mom and dad the best present you could ever give them. Can you guess what it is? The Bible says it's you! God gave you to them!

For MOM

For Dad

153

Song

Happy birthday to you
Happy birthday to you
Happy birthday dear _____
Happy birthday to you!

Verse to Remember

"Children are a gift

from the Lord."

Psalm 127:3

God Made Me

When you look in the mirror, what do you see? Yes, you see yourself! You move your arm, and your arm in the mirror moves. You make a funny face, and so does your face in the mirror. There's no way you can move your body in *front* of the mirror without your body moving *in* the mirror.

LORD, you have seen what is in my heart. You know all about me. LORD, even before I speak a word, you know all about it. You planned how many days I would live . . . before I had lived through even one of them.

Psalm 139:1, 4, 16

Read All About It: Psalm 139:1–18

Think about God as being kind of like that mirror. When you move your arm, he knows you moved your arm. When you move your head, he knows that too. God knows everything about you. He knows what you're going to say before you say it.

He knows what you're going to read before you read it! You see, God made you into the person you are. He created you. And he loves you. So you should love you too!

Song

(Traditional)

(God made my) Head and shoulders,
   knees and toes
Knees and toes, knees and toes,
Head and shoulders, knees and toes,
Eyes, ears, mouth, and nose.

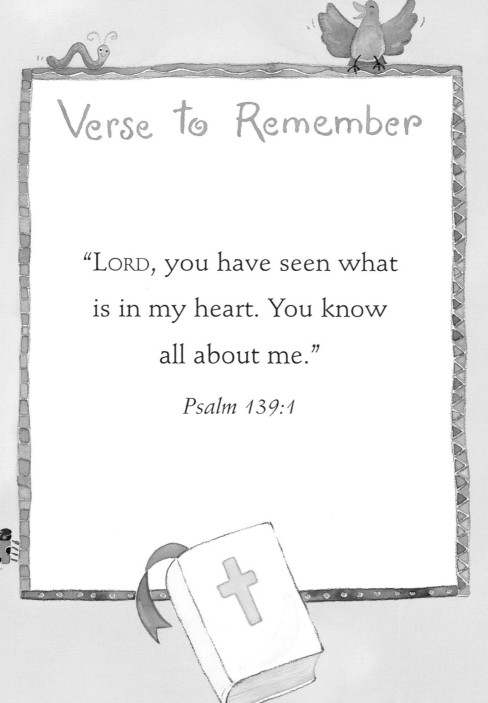

Verse to Remember

"LORD, you have seen what
is in my heart. You know
all about me."

Psalm 139:1

Smile!

Imagine that you and your family are getting ready to have your picture taken. The photographer tells a funny joke and, before you know it, you are all laughing! *Ha ha ha, hee hee hee.* Oh, it's so fun to laugh. When you laugh, you can't help but smile.

"A cheerful look brings joy to your heart."

Proverbs 15:30

Smiling is a wonderful thing. It's a good way to show other people that you are happy. If people who aren't having a very good day see you smile at them, they might begin to feel better. Then they might smile too. Try it!

Idea

Give a big, bright smile to the very next person you see today.

Verse to Remember

"A cheerful look brings joy
to your heart."

Proverbs 15:30

Grandpa and Grandma

Some of us are lucky enough to have grandpas and grandmas who live nearby. What are some fun things you like to do with them? How about going to a park and swinging on the swings, or spending a day at the zoo? How about going to the ice cream shop for hot fudge sundaes? Maybe you even get to sleep overnight at their house sometimes. What fun!

Grandchildren are like a crown to older people.

Proverbs 17:6

The Bible says that you are a wonderful gift to your grandparents. That's why you should spend time with your family, including your grandpa and grandma. Even if they live far away, you will probably be able to visit them and be together sometimes. And guess what? Your grandpa and grandma like to spend time with you as much as you like to spend time with them!

171

Idea

With your mom or dad's help, write your grandpa
and grandma a letter. Tell them what you like
to do with them and that you love them. Then
put the letter in an envelope with a stamp on it,
and drop it in the mailbox.

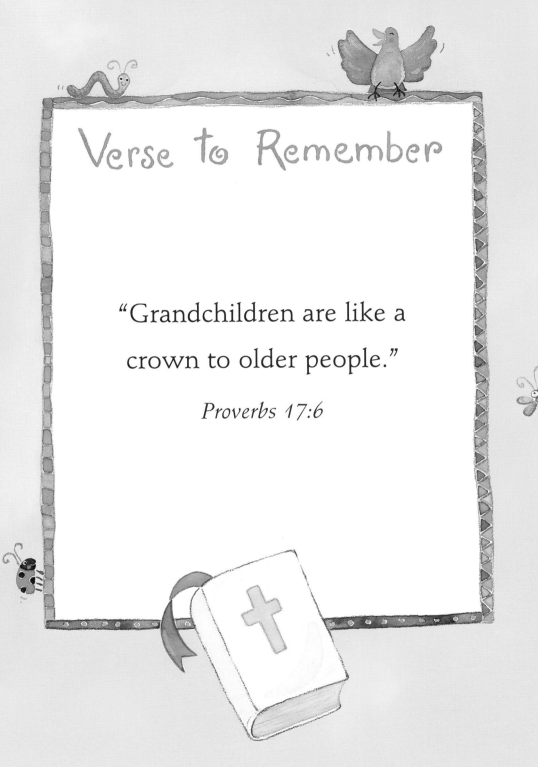

Verse to Remember

"Grandchildren are like a crown to older people."

Proverbs 17:6

Daniel and the Lions' Den

It's exciting to see lions at the zoo or at the circus. They are so big and so fierce and so beautiful! Their tails swish back and forth as they walk on their big paws. But we wouldn't want to go inside a lion's house, and we wouldn't want a real lion to go inside our house.

[Some leaders said to King Darius,] "Don't let any of your people pray to any god or man except to you. If they do, throw them into the lions' den." Daniel . . . went to his room three times a day to pray. Daniel was brought out and thrown into the lions' den. [The next day Daniel told the king,] "My God sent his angel. And his angel shut the mouths of the lions."

Daniel 6:7,10,16,22

Read All About It:
Daniel 6:1–28

In this Bible story, Daniel was thrown into a lions' den. No cages or bars kept Daniel safe from the lions. They swished their tails back and forth as they walked on their big paws around Daniel. But Daniel was not scared. God sent an angel to keep the lions' mouths shut so they wouldn't hurt Daniel. God knew that Daniel needed his help. And God saved Daniel from danger.

God can help us too when we feel
scared. All we need to do is pray to God
and ask for his help.

Idea

Roar like a lion! Now have someone pretend he or she is an angel. As soon as the angel touches your mouth, stop roaring.

Verse to Remember

"'My God sent his angel.
And his angel shut the
mouths of the lions.'"

Daniel 6:22

Time Out

When we do something that's bad, we sometimes have to take a "time out." Maybe we have to sit in a chair, or go to our room. "Time outs" give us a chance to think about what we did wrong and remember what's right. We wait and wait . . . and finally the time's up! Then we try to do what's right.

The LORD sent a huge fish to swallow Jonah. And Jonah was inside the fish for three days and three nights. From inside the fish Jonah prayed to the LORD his God. The Lord gave the fish a command. And it spit Jonah up onto dry land.

Jonah 1:17—2:1, 10

Read All About It: Jonah 1:17–2:10

In this Bible story, God gave a "time out" to a man named Jonah. But Jonah didn't have to sit in a chair or go to his room. After he disobeyed God, Jonah spent his "time out" in the belly of a fish! That's right. A big fish swallowed Jonah whole. *Gulp!*

From inside the fish's stomach, Jonah prayed that God would let him get out. He promised to do what was right, if only he could get out of that fish! Finally, after three days went by, God made the fish spit Jonah out onto dry land. Then Jonah obeyed God. Wouldn't you?

Idea

Lay on the floor and cover yourself with a blanket. Then imagine that you are Jonah in the belly of the fish. Is it dark? It is quiet? Is it lonely? After a few minutes, get up and go wherever you want to go in the house. Which did you like doing better and why?

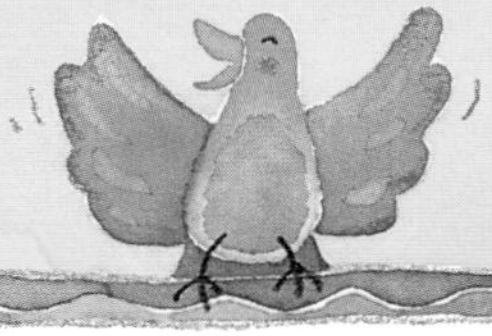

Verse to Remember

"From inside the fish
Jonah prayed to the
LORD his God."

Jonah 2:1

Baby Jesus and Me

There once was a girl who, at Christmas time, loved to sleep on the couch and watch the twinkling lights of the Christmas tree. Her mom would often wrap a quilt around her on those special nights. They would sit next to each other and talk for a long time. Sometimes the girl would ask her mom to tell her a story.

While Joseph and Mary were [in Bethlehem], the time came for the child to be born. She gave birth to her first baby. It was a boy. She wrapped him in large strips of cloth. Then she placed him in a manger. There was no room for them in the inn.

Luke 2:6–7

Read All About It:
Luke 2:1–7

One of the stories her mother would tell was about the night baby Jesus was born: "He had no bed like you—only a manger," the girl's mom would say. "He had no house like you—only a stable. He saw no Christmas tree like you—only the twinkling stars in the night sky. But he did have a mother who loved him very, very much, just like I love you. I'm sure Jesus' mommy tucked baby Jesus in at night like I do for you. 'Goodnight, Baby Jesus. Goodnight.'"

Song

Away in a manger, no crib for a bed,

The little Lord Jesus lay down his sweet head.

The stars in the sky looked down where he lay,

The little Lord Jesus asleep on the hay.

Stanza 1, anonymous
Music, James Ramsey Murray, 1887

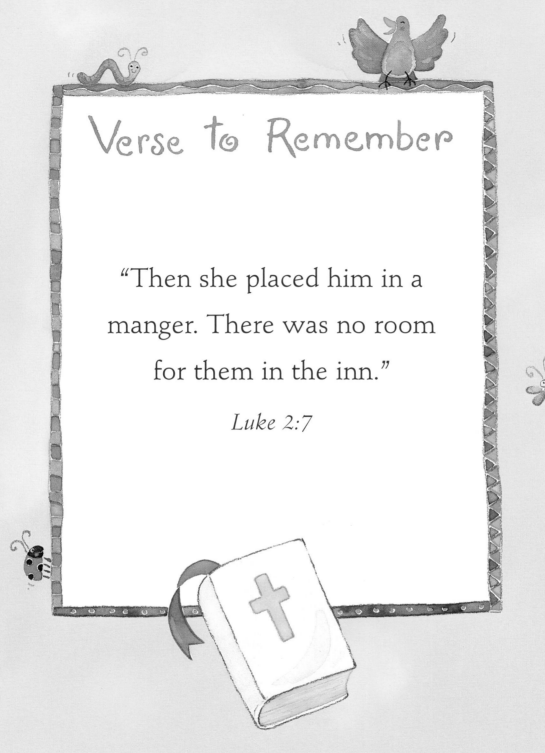

Verse to Remember

"Then she placed him in a manger. There was no room for them in the inn."

Luke 2:7

How to Go to Heaven

Look at the little boy in the picture. He is doing something nice for his grandma. He is getting her some soup for her lunch. How nice of him to do that!

Some people think that doing good things is what allows them to get to heaven. But the Bible says that believing in Jesus is the only way to get to heaven.

"God loved the world so much that he gave his one and only Son. Anyone who believes in him will not die but will have eternal life."

John 3:16

Jesus answered, "I am the way and truth and the life. No one comes to the Father except through me."

John 14:6

The most important part about being a Christian is believing that Jesus died to save us from our sins and then rose up from the dead. Yes, God is happy when we do good things for other people. But God wants us to love him above all, and believe that Jesus died to save us from our sins.

When we trust in Jesus and believe that he loves us, we know that our sins will be forgiven. Then when our life on earth is over, we will go to heaven.

Prayer

Dear God,
It's not the good things that I do
that will allow me to go to heaven some day.
   I'll go to heaven because I believe in you,
      and because I know that Jesus
      died and rose again to save
      me from my sins.
     God, please help me to do
       what's right every day,
        just because I know how
         much it pleases you.
    I thank you that someday,
     I will see you in heaven.

       Amen.

Verse to Remember

"Anyone who believes in [Jesus] will not die but will have eternal life."

John 3:16

The Lord's Prayer

When we close our eyes and fold our hands, what are we getting ready to do? Yes, we are getting ready to pray. Often we pray at the table before a meal or right before we go to bed. We say all sorts of different things to God when we pray.

[Jesus said,] This is how you should pray. "Our Father in heaven, may your name be honored. May your kingdom come. May what you want to happen be done on earth as it is done in heaven. Give us today our daily bread . . ."

Matthew 6:9–11

Read All About It: Matthew 6:5–15

When Jesus lived in the world long ago, he prayed to God often. He said that praying is very important for us to do. He taught us a prayer that is called the Lord's Prayer. Let's say it together:

Our Father in heaven,
hallowed be your name,
your kingdom come
your will be done
on earth as it is in heaven.
Give us this day
Our daily bread

Forgive us our debts,
as we also have forgiven
our debtors.
And lead us not into temptation
But deliver us from the evil one.
For yours is the kingdom
and the power
and the glory forever.
Amen.

NIV

Idea

Practice saying the Lord's Prayer with your mom or dad. Pick a certain time of day when you say it; perhaps right before you go to bed at night.

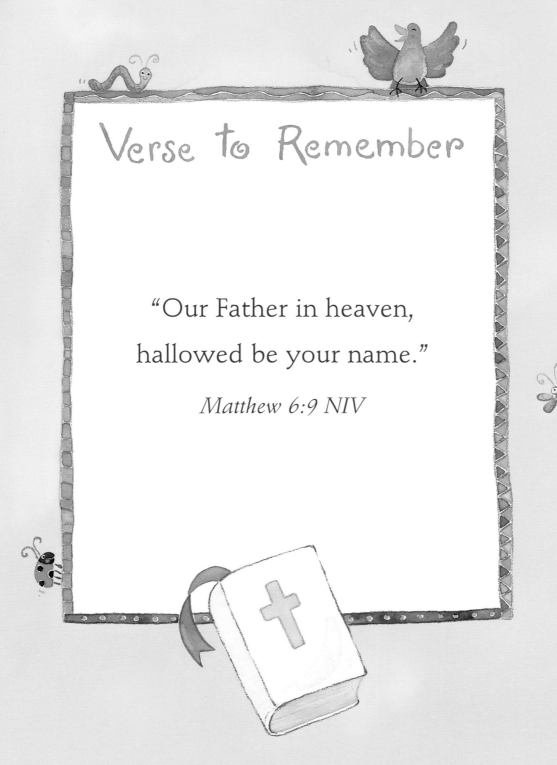

Verse to Remember

"Our Father in heaven,
hallowed be your name."

Matthew 6:9 NIV

I Don't Need to Worry

"What are we going to do today?" "Where is my favorite toy?" "When will you read me a story?" "Am I going to have to go to bed soon?"

Have you ever asked any of these questions? You want to know everything that's going to happen. But you don't need to worry. Jesus doesn't want you to worry.

Don't worry about your life and what you will eat or drink. Look at the birds of the air. They don't plant or gather crops. But your Father who is in heaven feeds them. Put God's kingdom first. Do what he wants you to do. Then all of those things will also be given to you.

Matthew 6:25–26, 33

Read All About It: Matthew 6:25–34

Jesus said to look at the birds. They sing and tweet and fly up in the air. They don't have refrigerators or kitchens to store food in. But they never worry about when they'll eat dinner—not even a little bit. Do you know why? Because God takes care of them.

Yes, God loves the birds. And he loves you too! If God can take care of the birds outside, how much more will he take care of you? Lots and lots! So, don't worry. Instead, remember to look at the birds!

Idea

Pretend that you are a bird. Flap your wings and sing, "Tweet, tweet." You could even eat some cereal and pretend it is birdseed!

tweet
tweet

Verse to Remember

"But put God's kingdom first. Do what he wants you to do."

Matthew 6:33

Sandcastles

Imagine making the very tip-top tower of a big sandcastle at the beach in the summertime. People gather around and tell you what a good job you've done. You look out over the water and see a big wave coming onto shore. Oh no! What's going to happen to your sandcastle? *Whoosh!* In comes the wave, and down goes your sandcastle.

[Jesus said,] "Everyone who hears my words and puts them into practice is like a wise man. He builds his house on the rock. The rain comes down. The water rises. The winds blow and beat against that house. But it does not fall. It is built on the rock.

Matthew 7:24–25

Read All About It:
Matthew 7:24–29

Now think about your own house. It does not fall when the rains come down on it. Jesus said that people who love him and do what he says are like your house. No matter what happens around them, they will be safe in Jesus' love. But people who don't do what Jesus says are like the sand-castle. When tough times come, they will not be safe in Jesus' love.

Idea

Pretend you are a house on the sand. The rain comes down and the wind blows . . . and you fall down! Now pretend that you are a house on the rock. The rain comes down and the wind blows . . . and you stay standing. Hooray! That's what it's like to be safe in Jesus' love.

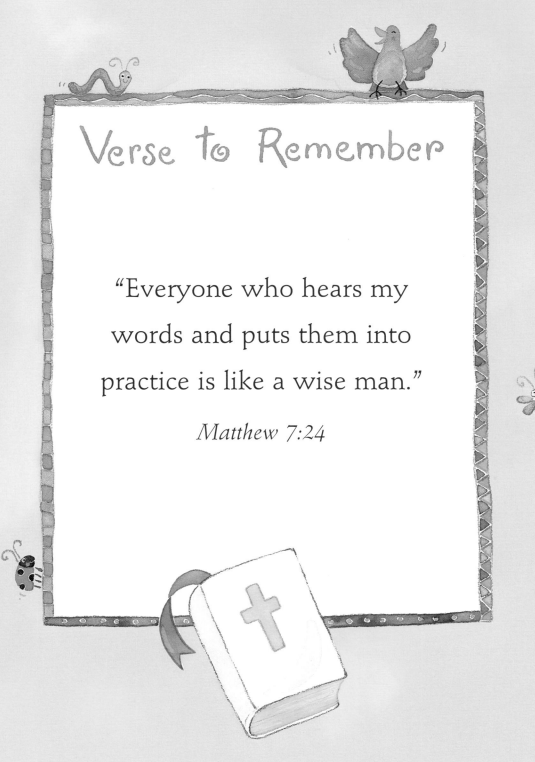

Verse to Remember

"Everyone who hears my words and puts them into practice is like a wise man."

Matthew 7:24

216

When I'm Afraid

Not many people like thunderstorms. The rain comes down from the sky. It sounds like little hammers hitting the roof—*bang, bang . . . bang, bang, bang!* The sun hides behind the gloomy sky. The wind whooshes outside, and when you look out the window you see tree branches bending back and forth, back and forth. Thunderstorms can be scary!

The disciples . . . said, "Lord! Save us! We're going to drown!" He replied, "Your faith is so small! Why are you so afraid?" Then Jesus got up and ordered the winds and the waves to stop. It became completely calm. The disciples were amazed.
Matthew 8:23–27

When I'm afraid, I will trust in you.
Psalm 56:3

Read All About It:
Matthew 8:18–27

Some friends of Jesus didn't like thunderstorms either. They were riding on a boat when, suddenly, rain came down from the sky. The boat swayed back and forth, back and forth as the wind whipped up the waves. "Jesus, help us! Our boat is going to sink!" they cried.

Jesus lifted his hands and told the storm to be quiet. Right away the rain stopped falling from the sky. The sun came back out. The whooshing wind was still. The boat stopped swaying back and forth.

Isn't Jesus amazing?

Idea

To remember this story, draw a picture of Jesus standing in the boat with calm water all around. Be sure to draw in the disciples' smiling faces! The next time you're afraid, remember this drawing. Jesus can help you.

Verse to Remember

"Then Jesus got up and ordered the winds and the waves to stop. It became completely calm."

Matthew 8:26

Nothing Is Too Hard for Jesus

Have you ever been to a hospital? People go to the hospital for different reasons. Some go there to have babies. Other people go there because they have been hurt. Still others go there because they are sick. The doctors and nurses try to help these people get well. Many people get better, but some people don't.

Someone came from the house of Jairus. "Your daughter is dead," the messenger said. Jesus said to Jairus, "Don't be afraid. Just believe. She will be healed." When he arrived at the house of Jairus . . . [Jesus] took her by the hand and said, "My child, get up!" Her spirit returned, and right away she stood up.

Luke 8:49–51, 54–55

Read All About It:
Luke 8:40–56

In this Bible story, a man named Jairus had a daughter who was very sick. Jairus believed that Jesus could help his daughter get better. But by the time he found Jesus, his daughter had already died. Oh, how sad this father was! But it wasn't too late. Jesus went to Jairus's house, and he brought the little girl back to life. It was a miracle!

When Jesus lived on earth, he helped a lot of sick people get better. He even brought people back to life, like this little girl. Jesus, God's Son, is the best healer of all time.

Idea

Do you know someone who is sick? Write that person a card and draw a picture on the front of it. Pray to Jesus and ask him to help this person get better.

Verse to Remember

"Don't be afraid.
Just believe. She will
be healed."

Luke 8:50

Jesus Did a Miracle!

One day when a little girl went to preschool, she forgot to take her lunch box. She wondered, "How will I make it through the day without eating anything?" When lunchtime came, some of her classmates helped her. One boy gave her half of a peanut butter sandwich. One girl gave her a bright red apple. Her teacher gave her some milk to drink. They all shared. And they all had enough to eat that day!

Jesus . . . said, "Where can we buy bread for these people to eat?" Andrew . . . said, "Here is a boy with five small loaves of barley bread. He also has two small fish. But how far will that go in such a large crowd?" Then Jesus took the loaves and gave thanks. He gave [the people] as much as they wanted.

John 6:5, 8–9, 11

Read All About It:
John 6:1–15

229

In this Bible story, a boy shared his lunch with Jesus. The people who had been listening to Jesus were getting hungry. This boy had a lunch, but in it were only five bread loaves and two fish. He gave all of his food to Jesus.

Then Jesus made a miracle happen! From that little boy's lunch, he made enough lunch for everyone. All the people had plenty to eat that day—all 5,000 of them!

Idea

The next time you eat something, share half of it with someone else. Then tell them the story of the little boy who shared, and the miracle Jesus did with that food.

Verse to Remember

"Then Jesus took the loaves
and gave thanks."

John 6:11

Helping Others

One day at a park, a little girl saw a boy fall off a swing. His knee was scraped, and he started to cry. Some people saw what happened, but they didn't help the boy. The girl walked over to him and helped him up. Then she got a Band-Aid® from her mom to cover the scrape. The boy knew that the girl cared about him, even though she didn't know him.

Robbers attacked [a man] . . . leaving him almost dead. [When] a priest . . . saw the man, he passed by on the other side. A Levite . . . passed by on the other side too. When [a Samaritan] saw the man, he felt sorry for him. He took him to an inn and took care of him.

Luke 10:30–34

Read All About It:
Luke 10:25–37

In this Bible story, a Samaritan saw a man lying by the side of the road. This man needed help. The Samaritan could have ignored the man. After all, two other people had walked by without helping. But he stopped. The Samaritan put the hurt man on his donkey and brought him to a place where he could get better.

When we see people who need help, we must think about what Jesus would want us to do. And then we must do it!

Idea

Pretend that one of your stuffed animals
is hurt. Be a good Samaritan to it.

Verse to Remember

"When [a Samaritan] saw the man, he felt sorry for him. He took him to an inn and took care of him."

Luke 10:33–34

Busy Busy Busy!

What kinds of things do you do during the day? If you're like most children, you wake up in the morning and eat breakfast, brush your teeth, and maybe play with your toys. If you're old enough, you go to school. Then you play outside with your friends, and ride your bike if the weather's nice. In the evening you eat supper and have playtime with your family. Finally, you go to bed. What a busy, busy day!

[Martha] came to Jesus and said, "Lord, my sister has left me to do the work by myself. Don't you care? Tell her to help me!" "Martha, Martha," the Lord answered. "You are worried and upset about many things. But only one thing is needed. Mary has chosen what is better."

Luke 10:40–41

Read All About It: Luke 10:38–42

In this Bible story, Martha had very busy days, just like you do. She went here and there, always working. But her sister Mary liked to sit still sometimes and think about things. One day Jesus came to their house for a visit. Martha was busy, but Mary sat still and listened to Jesus. And Jesus said that Mary was doing the right thing by taking time to be quiet.

We may need to be busy sometimes, but let's always make time to sit still and think about Jesus.

Idea

Play the game "Duck, Duck, Goose,"
but say "Mary, Mary, Martha" instead.

Verse to Remember

"'Martha, Martha,' the Lord
answered. 'You are worried
and upset about many
things. But only one thing is
needed. Mary has chosen
what is better.'"

Luke 10:41

I'm Lost!

There once was a girl who often went to the store with her mom. They had fun shopping for all kinds of things. One time, in the middle of seeing this and seeing that, the girl looked up and discovered—Oh no!—she was lost! But soon her mom came around the corner. The worried looks on their faces turned into smiles when they saw each other again.

"Suppose one of you has 100 sheep and loses one of them. Won't he leave the 99 in the open country? Won't he go and look for the one lost sheep until he finds it? When he finds it, he . . . will say, 'Be joyful with me. I have found my lost sheep.'"

Luke 15:4–6

Read All About It:
Luke 15:4-6

This story reminds us of a passage in the Bible about sheep. Sheep love to run and prance in green fields—*Baa, baa.* What fun it is to prance and play! Sometimes sheep look up and discover—Oh no!—they are lost! But soon their shepherd goes out and finds them.

God knows where everybody is all of the time. If we ask him, he can help us find each other when we get lost. All we need to do is trust that he will help.

Prayer

The Lord is my shepherd,
And I am his sheep.
He watches over me
Even when I sleep.

Watch over me, Lord
As I prance and play.
Watch over me, Lord,
By night and by day.

Amen.

Verse to Remember

"Be joyful with me. I have found my lost sheep."

Luke 15:6

I'm Sorry

One day, a little boy took his crayons and scribbled up and down the family room wall. When he tried to clean off the wall, the crayon just smeared. "What will I do now?" he worried. Tears filled his eyes.

The little boy went to his dad and told him he was sorry. His dad was not happy about the crayon marks. But he was glad that his little boy felt sorry. He loved him so much!

The father divided his property between his two sons. The younger son . . . wasted his money on wild living. He spent everything he had. He said . . . "I will get up and go back to my father. I will say to him, 'Father . . . I have sinned against you.'" His father . . . ran to him. He threw his arms around him and kissed him.

Luke 15:12, 13–14, 17–20

Read All About It:
Luke 15:11–31

This Bible story is about a young man who did some wrong things. He left his home and went far away and wasted all of his money. Then he went back to his house to tell his dad that he was sorry for what he had done. But before he got there, his dad ran out to meet him. Oh, was he glad his son had come back to say he was sorry. He loved his son so much!

Prayer

I'm sorry, Jesus, that I sinned.
Please forgive me, I pray.
Guide me so I know what to do
Today, tomorrow and always.

Amen.

Verse to Remember

"His father . . . ran to him.
He threw his arms around
him and kissed him."

Luke 15:20

Thank You!

When we feel sick, it's really hard to be happy because we can't do all the things we love to do. Sometimes we are sick for a long time. But when we start to feel better, we want to jump up and down because we're so happy!

As [Jesus] was going into a village, ten men met him. They had a skin disease. Jesus saw them and said, "Go. Show yourselves to the priests." When one of them saw that he was healed, he came back. He praised God in a loud voice. Jesus asked, "Weren't all ten healed? Where are the other nine?"

Luke 17:12–18

Read All About It: Luke 17:11–19

In Bible times, some people used to get sick with sores all over their bodies. One day Jesus saw ten men who were sick with this skin disease. Jesus felt sorry for them. Can you guess what he did? He healed them. All of their sores disappeared! They could now go back to their homes, their families, and their work. They probably jumped up and down because they were so happy! But, as happy as they were, only one man came back to praise God.

We need to remember to pray to God too and thank him for making us feel better after we've been sick.

Idea

Jump up and down five times. Each time
you jump, say, "Thank you, Jesus!"

Verse to Remember

"When one of them saw that he was healed, he came back. He praised God in a loud voice."

Luke 17:15

Jesus Loves Me

There once was a boy and a girl who loved to welcome their dad home from work. They would rush to the door and say, "Daddy, Daddy" this and "Daddy, Daddy" that. Their daddy would scoop them up in his arms and then sit with them snuggled into his lap. How wonderful they felt in their daddy's arms. He would look at his happy children, and his eyes would twinkle with tender love for them.

Some people brought little children to Jesus. They wanted him to place his hands on the children and pray for them. But the disciples told the people to stop. Jesus said, "Let the little children come to me. Don't keep them away. The kingdom of heaven belongs to people like them."

Matthew 19:13–14

Read All About It:
Matthew 19:13–15

In this Bible story, the children felt the same way about Jesus. They were so glad to see him. They probably rushed to his side and said, "Jesus, Jesus" this and "Jesus, Jesus" that. He probably scooped them up and then sat with them snuggled into his lap. How wonderful they must have felt in Jesus' arms. As he looked at all the happy children, his eyes must have twinkled with tender love for them.

Jesus loves you too!

Song

Jesus loves me, this I know,

For the Bible tells me so.

Little ones to him belong,

They are weak, but he is strong.

Yes, Jesus loves me (3 times),

The Bible tells me so.

Stanza 1, Anna Bartlett Warner, 1860
Music, William Batchelder Bradbury, 1862

Verse to Remember

"Jesus said, 'Let the little children come to me. Don't keep them away.'"

Matthew 19:14

I Wish I Were Taller!

Have you ever wished you were taller? Then you wouldn't have to drink out of the lower drinking fountain. You could push the shopping cart around the store instead of riding in it! Don't worry, you're still growing.

Zacchaeus wanted to see who Jesus was. But he was a short man. So he ran ahead and climbed a sycamore-fig tree. Jesus reached the spot where Zacchaeus was. He looked up and said, "Zacchaeus, come down at once. I must stay at your house today."

Luke 19:3–5

Read All About It:
Luke 19:1–9

Zacchaeus was a very short man. Because of his job, people weren't nice to him. Zacchaeus wanted to see Jesus. But too many people stood in the way. So you know what he did? He climbed up into a tree! Jesus saw him up in the tree and said to Zacchaeus, "I must stay at your house today."

Jesus doesn't look at how short or how tall we are. He loves short people and tall people. He loves older people and young children. And he wants us to be kind to each other.

Song

(Traditional)

Zacchaeus was a wee little man,

And a wee little man was he.

He climbed up in a sycamore tree,

For the Lord he wanted to see.

And as the Savior passed
that way,

He looked up in the tree.

And he said, "Zacchaeus,
you come down."

For I'm going to your house today,

For I'm going to your house today.

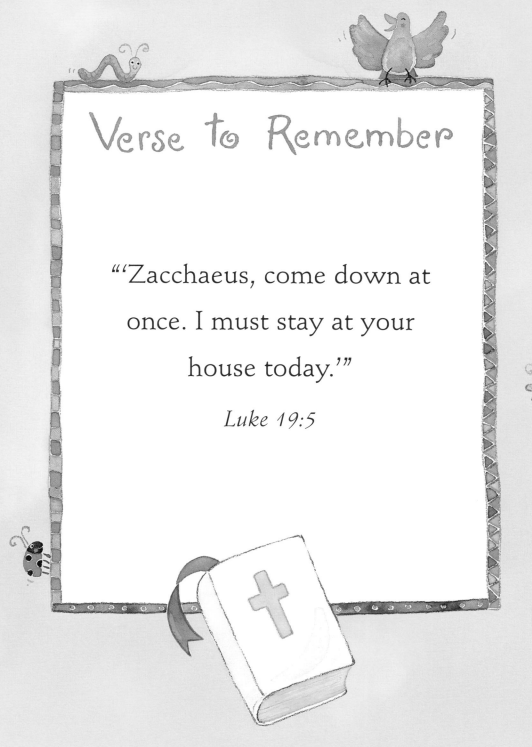

Verse to Remember

"'Zacchaeus, come down at once. I must stay at your house today.'"

Luke 19:5

Jesus Died to Pay for My Sins

Bath time is fun time! As the water streams out from the faucet and tumbles into the tub, you climb in. *Splish splash . . . kersploosh!* You scrub-scrub-scrub and guess what? Your body is clean again! All the dirt on your body has washed off into the water.

[Christ died for sins once and for all time. The One who did what is right died for those who don't do right. He died to bring you to God. His body was put to death. But the Holy Spirit brought him back to life.

1 Peter 3:18

Read All About It:
1 Peter 3:16–18, 21–22

277

It feels great to be clean on the outside, but it feels even better to be clean on the inside. In other words, it feels great when we know our sins are forgiven. But how can we be forgiven for all the bad things we do and say?

Through Jesus! Jesus is God's very own Son. He lived on this earth, and he did a wonderful, incredible thing. Jesus died for us on a cross. He paid for all our sins. He went through a lot of pain, and he even gave up his life for us. But there's a happy ending. Read the next Bible story to find out what happened.

Idea

The next time you're done with your bath, look at the dirty water and imagine that it is your sins. Then pull the plug and watch the water drain out of the tub. Think about Jesus as being like that drain, taking your sins away.

Verse to Remember

"Christ died for sins
once and for all time."

1 Peter 3:18

Jesus Is Alive!

When people want flowers to come up in the spring, they plant seeds in the ground. The seeds don't look alive. They are brown and hard. They don't look like flowers at all. But then in the spring, up come the flowers. How beautiful and alive they are!

An angel of the Lord came down from heaven. He rolled back the stone and sat on it. His body shone like lightning. The angel said to the women, "Don't be afraid. I know that you are looking for Jesus, who was crucified. He is not here! He has risen, just as he said he would!"

Matthew 28:1–6

Read All About It:
Matthew 28:1–20

Now think about Jesus. After Jesus died, he was buried. People put him in a tomb and rolled a huge stone in front of it. They thought Jesus was gone forever. But three days later, Jesus came out from the tomb. The angel rolled the stone away. Jesus was alive again!

When Jesus rose from the dead and left the tomb, he set us free from our sins. That's the most wonderful news in the whole Bible!

Song

"Christ the Lord is risen today," Alleluia!

Sons of men and angels say; Alleluia!

Raise your joys and triumphs high; Alleluia!

Sing, you heavens, and earth reply. Alleluia!

Stanza 1, Charles Wesley, 1739
Music, "Easter Hymn," Lyra Davidica, *1708*

Verse to Remember

"He is not here!
He has risen, just as
he said he would!"

Matthew 28:6

Jesus Goes to Heaven

Have you ever played the game "pass it on"? One person tells someone a message. Then that person tells another person, until the message has gone all the way around a circle of people. The last person who gets the message says what the message is. It's a fun game!

Jesus appeared to the [disciples]. He said to them, "Go into all the world. Preach the good news to everyone. Anyone who believes and is baptized will be saved. But anyone who does not believe will be punished." When the Lord Jesus finished speaking to them, he was taken up into heaven.

Mark 16:14–15, 19

Read All About It:
Mark 16:9–20

After Jesus rose from the dead, he told some women to pass on the message that he was alive. And they did! Later, Jesus appeared to the disciples. Jesus knew he wouldn't be on the earth much longer. He was soon going back to heaven. So Jesus gave his friends a message and asked them

to "pass it on." Jesus' followers told others about Jesus so they could learn about Jesus and become Christians too.

Are you a follower of Jesus? Do you love him like his disciples did? Then he wants you to "pass on" the message too. With God's help, others can become Christians too.

Idea

Play the "pass it on" game with your family.
Say, "Jesus loves you! Pass it on!"

Verse to Remember

"Go into all the world.
Preach the good news
to everyone."

Mark 16:15

Jesus Will Come Back

Do you remember your last visit with your grandparents? They packed up their things and kissed you goodbye. Maybe you stood outside and waved as they drove away. If your grandparents live close by, you probably weren't very sad. You knew you'd see them again soon. But if they live very far away, you may have been very sad to see them go.

Jesus . . . was taken up to heaven. Suddenly two men dressed in white clothing stood beside them. "Men of Galilee," they said, "why do you stand there looking at the sky? Jesus has been taken away from you into heaven. But he will come back in the same way you saw him go."

Acts 1:9–11

Read All About It:
Acts 1:3–11

The people in this Bible story had to say goodbye to Jesus. A big cloud came down and took Jesus up into the sky. Two angels told the people who were watching not to worry. They promised that Jesus would come back to earth someday. And when he came back, he would come in the same way he left.

When he comes again, Jesus will take all
of his people—all Christians from around
the world—to heaven to be with him.
What a wonderful day that will be!

Song

Jesus loves the little children,
All the children of the world—
Red and yellow black and white,
They are precious in his sight.
Jesus loves the little children of
the world.

Words, C. H. Woolston
Music, George Frederick Root (1820-1895)

Verse to Remember

"'Jesus has been taken
away from you into
heaven. But he will come
back in the same way
you saw him go.'"

Acts 1:11

Jesus Changes Saul

We all know that some people in the world do really bad things. Some people steal money from banks. Some people are in gangs that kill people. Some people burn down churches. But even people who do really bad things can be changed into good people. God can turn anyone into a good person, no matter how bad he or she used to be.

Suddenly a light from heaven flashed around [Saul]. He heard a voice speak to him. "Saul! Saul! . . . Why are you opposing me?" "Who are you, Lord?" Saul asked. "I am Jesus," he replied. "I am the one you are opposing." [After this, Saul] taught that Jesus is the Son of God. All who heard him were amazed.

Acts 9:3–5, 20–21

Read All About It: Acts 9:1–22

That's what happened to Saul in this Bible story. He was trying to hurt Christians just because they were Christians! But when he was walking on the road one day, a light suddenly flashed down from heaven all around him. When Jesus spoke to Saul from heaven, he changed how Saul felt about Christians. Saul didn't want to hurt Christians anymore. Instead, Saul wanted to *become* a Christian!

Saul changed his name to Paul. And, with his new name, Paul spent the rest of his life telling others about the Good News of Jesus.

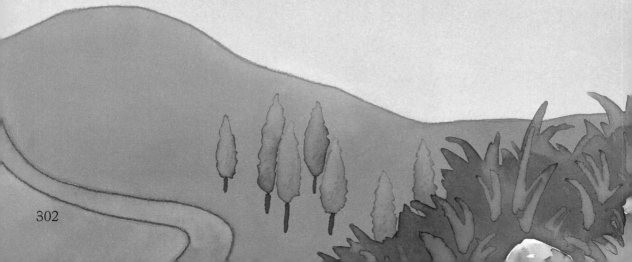

Question

What did Saul do when he was bad?
What did Paul do when he was good?

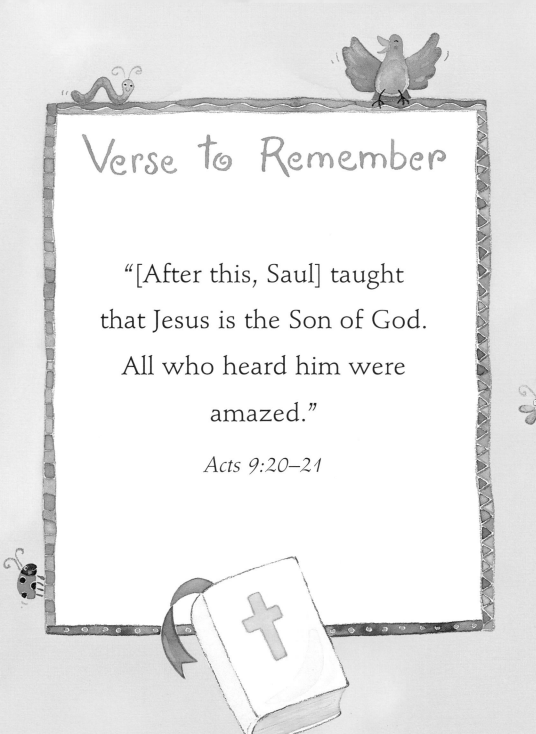

Verse to Remember

"[After this, Saul] taught that Jesus is the Son of God. All who heard him were amazed."

Acts 9:20–21

What Is Love?

Imagine that you are sleeping in your bed early in the morning. You hear someone's footsteps. You open your eyes, and you see your mom. She's smiling at you. You sit up in bed, and she wraps her arms around you. "Good morning, honey. I love you!" she says. You can't help but smile as you hug her back.

Love is patient. Love is kind. It always protects. It always trusts. It always hopes. It never gives up. Love never fails. The three most important things to have are faith, hope and love. But the greatest of them is love.

1 Corinthians 13:4, 7–8, 13

Read All About It:
1 Corinthians 13:1–13

Love is one of the best feelings a person can have. Different people feel love and show love in different ways. Maybe your mom doesn't wake you up in the morning. Maybe she cooks you a yummy breakfast instead. Or maybe she reads you your favorite story . . . twice in a row! When people love you, they want what's best for you. They want you to be happy. They will do just about anything for you.

Think about the people you love. How do you show them your love? And how do they show you their love?

Idea

Draw a picture for someone you love.
Then give it to that person and say,
"I love you!"

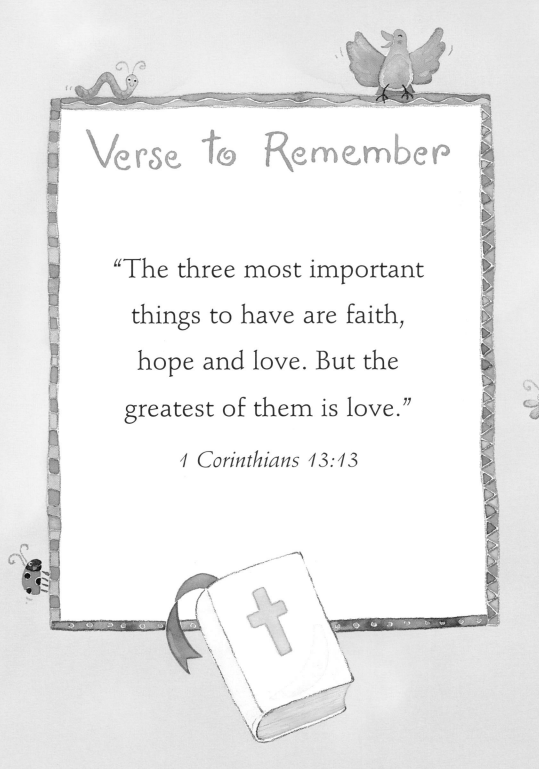

Verse to Remember

"The three most important things to have are faith, hope and love. But the greatest of them is love."

1 Corinthians 13:13

I Want to Share

There once was a boy who got a new toy truck. He loved it! He played with his truck in the sandbox. He washed it with the garden hose. He raced it down the driveway: *Zooom!* One day his cousin came over and asked to play with the new truck. But the boy didn't want to share. When his cousin tried to take the truck, the boy held it tightly.

"Don't forget to share with others."

Hebrews 13:16

Just then the boy's dad came outside. He said, "Hey boys, why not take turns playing with that truck?" So that's what the boy and his cousin did. They were having so much fun they didn't even see the dad come back outside and get in his real truck. But when he started his truck's engine— *Vroom! Vroom!*—the boys looked up with excitement. "Come on," the dad said. And off they went for a ride in the real thing!

Idea

The next time you play with a friend or with a brother or sister, share your favorite toys. See what happens!

Verse to Remember

"Don't forget to share
with others."

Hebrews 13:16

My Very First Devotional Bible

Written by Catherine DeVries

Interior and Cover Artwork by Leanne Mebust Luetkemeyer

Zondervan Art Direction and Design by Jody Langley

Zondervan Production by Mark Luce

Zondervan Editorial by Michael Vander Klipp

Interior Composition by Pamela J. L. Eicher

Catherine DeVries *is a senior editor in the Bible Group at Zondervan Publishing House. While this is Catherine's first children's book, her writings have appeared in various Zondervan Bibles, Bookstore Journal, and HarperCollins Life Magazine. She and her husband Brad live with their son Bryce and their dog Blitzen in Grandville, Michigan.*

Leanne Mebust Luetkemeyer *has a B.F.A. from the University of Kansas and has worked for more than eight years at Hallmark Cards. Currently a freelance illustrator, she lives with her husband in Boulder, CO.*